MELANIE
AND THE MAGIC BUBBLE

BY
MARY HOUGHTON DOCKSTEADER

In memory of my dear mother,
Ila Houghton

POLESTAR
BOOK PUBLISHERS

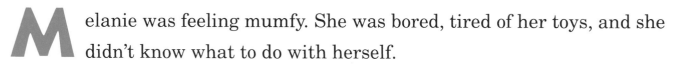**M**elanie was feeling mumfy. She was bored, tired of her toys, and she didn't know what to do with herself.

"Don't be mumfy," said her mother. "You have lots of things to play with."

"I wish you would play with me, Mommy."

"Well, perhaps in a little while, after I'm finished in the kitchen," and she turned and went back into the house.

So Melanie sighed a big sigh and sat like a lump on the front doorstep and waited. Ginger, her kitten, sat beside her and looked mumfy too.

Melanie looked up to see her neighbour, Mrs Huggins, coming down the sidewalk towards them.

"Goodness gracious, you do look sad," chuckled Mrs. Huggins.

"I don't have anything to do," said Melanie, staring glumly down at her shoes.

"Oh my, that won't do, will it!" and with that Mrs. Huggins reached deep down into her shopping bag and pulled out a small bottle. The label said in very tiny letters…

"This seems to be my very last bottle so you had better take care it doesn't spill. Now, if you blow bubbles from this very special bottle, perhaps you will have a change of heart. Now I'm off to the park to feed the birds," she said as she handed the bottle to Melanie.

"Well Ginger, there's nothing else to do. I guess we might as well try it."

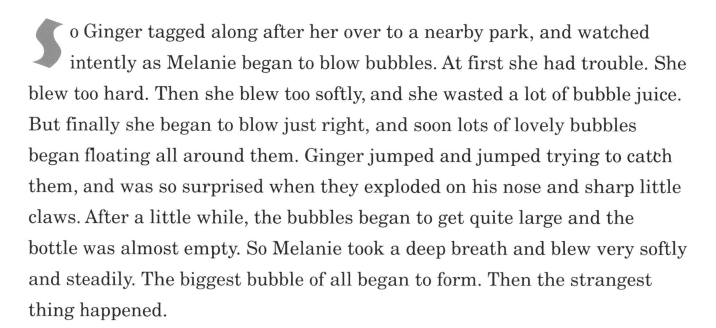

So Ginger tagged along after her over to a nearby park, and watched intently as Melanie began to blow bubbles. At first she had trouble. She blew too hard. Then she blew too softly, and she wasted a lot of bubble juice. But finally she began to blow just right, and soon lots of lovely bubbles began floating all around them. Ginger jumped and jumped trying to catch them, and was so surprised when they exploded on his nose and sharp little claws. After a little while, the bubbles began to get quite large and the bottle was almost empty. So Melanie took a deep breath and blew very softly and steadily. The biggest bubble of all began to form. Then the strangest thing happened.

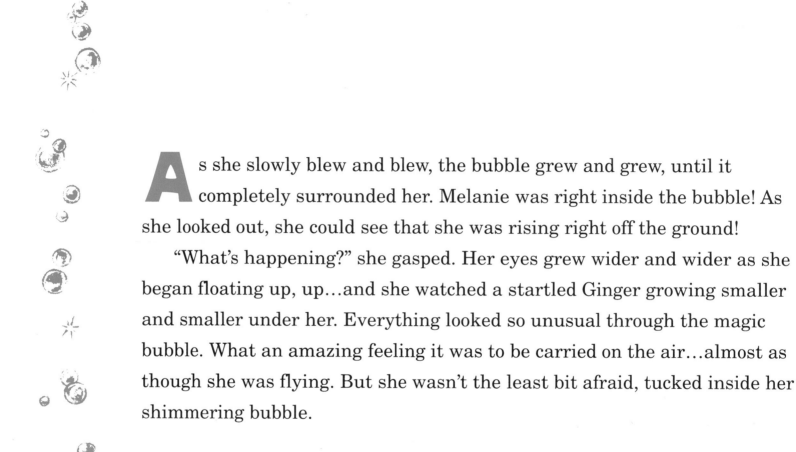

As she slowly blew and blew, the bubble grew and grew, until it completely surrounded her. Melanie was right inside the bubble! As she looked out, she could see that she was rising right off the ground!

"What's happening?" she gasped. Her eyes grew wider and wider as she began floating up, up…and she watched a startled Ginger growing smaller and smaller under her. Everything looked so unusual through the magic bubble. What an amazing feeling it was to be carried on the air…almost as though she was flying. But she wasn't the least bit afraid, tucked inside her shimmering bubble.

Higher and higher she went until she was floating over her own house. She had never really noticed it before, with the cheerful little garden in the back that her parents had planted. As she drifted over the houses, she spied Mrs. Huggins down below, sitting on a bench feeding birds.

"What a nice lady she is," thought Melanie, "she's always smiling and she smells just like cinnamon buns." She waved down at her and Mrs. Huggins smiled a secret smile and waved back.

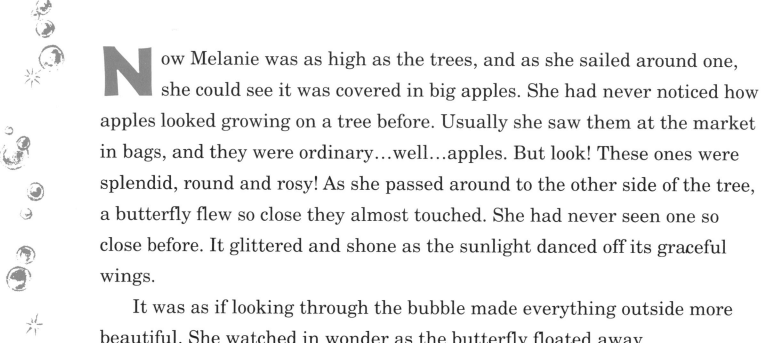

Now Melanie was as high as the trees, and as she sailed around one, she could see it was covered in big apples. She had never noticed how apples looked growing on a tree before. Usually she saw them at the market in bags, and they were ordinary…well…apples. But look! These ones were splendid, round and rosy! As she passed around to the other side of the tree, a butterfly flew so close they almost touched. She had never seen one so close before. It glittered and shone as the sunlight danced off its graceful wings.

It was as if looking through the bubble made everything outside more beautiful. She watched in wonder as the butterfly floated away.

Up and up Melanie went until she could see quite far below. "There's my school!" she cried, "and the mall, and Jackie's house, the park, and Mr. Brown's truck…wow, everything looks great!"

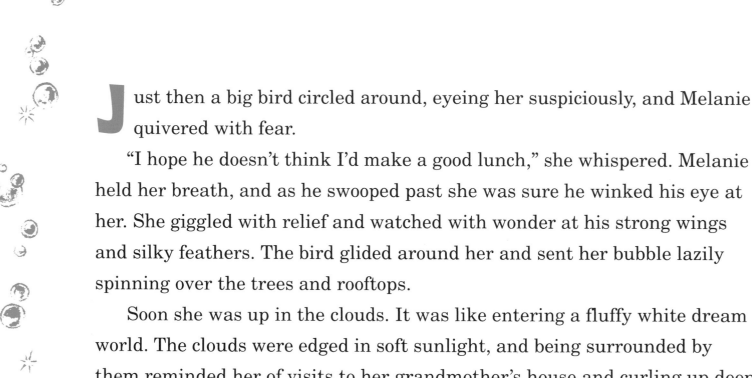

Just then a big bird circled around, eyeing her suspiciously, and Melanie quivered with fear.

"I hope he doesn't think I'd make a good lunch," she whispered. Melanie held her breath, and as he swooped past she was sure he winked his eye at her. She giggled with relief and watched with wonder at his strong wings and silky feathers. The bird glided around her and sent her bubble lazily spinning over the trees and rooftops.

Soon she was up in the clouds. It was like entering a fluffy white dream world. The clouds were edged in soft sunlight, and being surrounded by them reminded her of visits to her grandmother's house and curling up deep in her fleecy eiderdown quilt.

Suddenly she was very tired. Where was home?

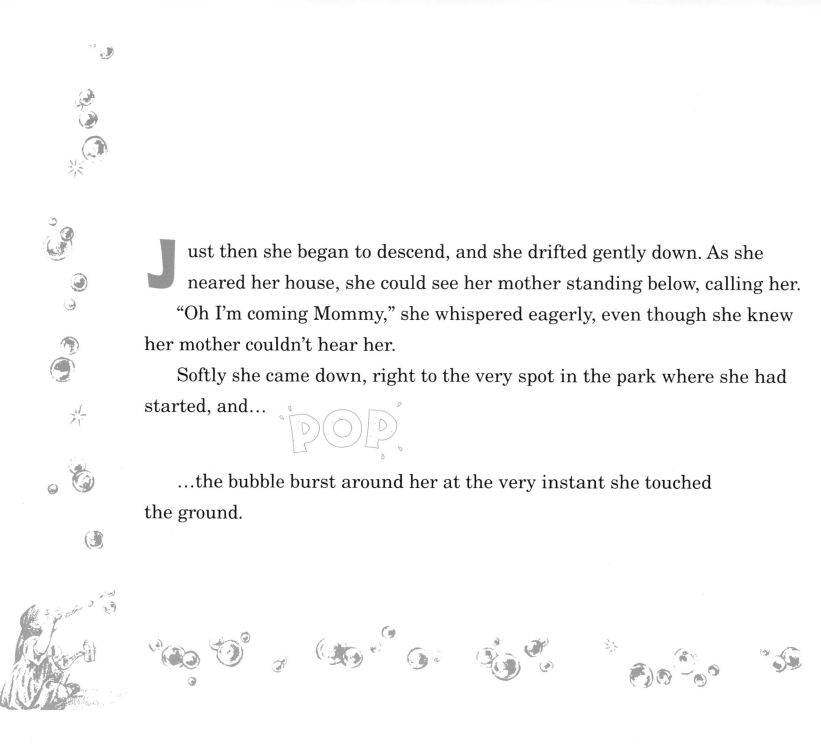

Just then she began to descend, and she drifted gently down. As she neared her house, she could see her mother standing below, calling her.

"Oh I'm coming Mommy," she whispered eagerly, even though she knew her mother couldn't hear her.

Softly she came down, right to the very spot in the park where she had started, and... POP

...the bubble burst around her at the very instant she touched the ground.

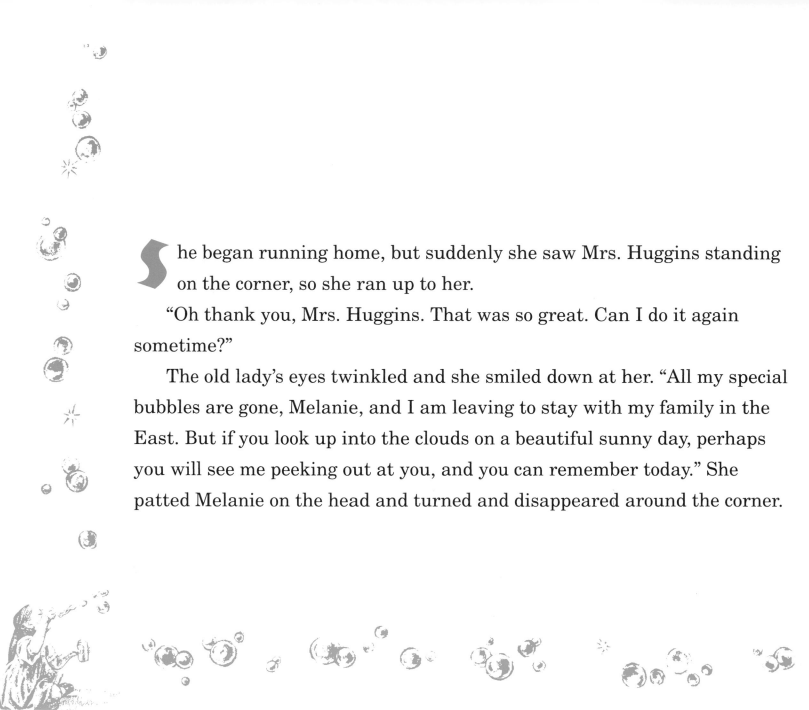

She began running home, but suddenly she saw Mrs. Huggins standing on the corner, so she ran up to her.

"Oh thank you, Mrs. Huggins. That was so great. Can I do it again sometime?"

The old lady's eyes twinkled and she smiled down at her. "All my special bubbles are gone, Melanie, and I am leaving to stay with my family in the East. But if you look up into the clouds on a beautiful sunny day, perhaps you will see me peeking out at you, and you can remember today." She patted Melanie on the head and turned and disappeared around the corner.

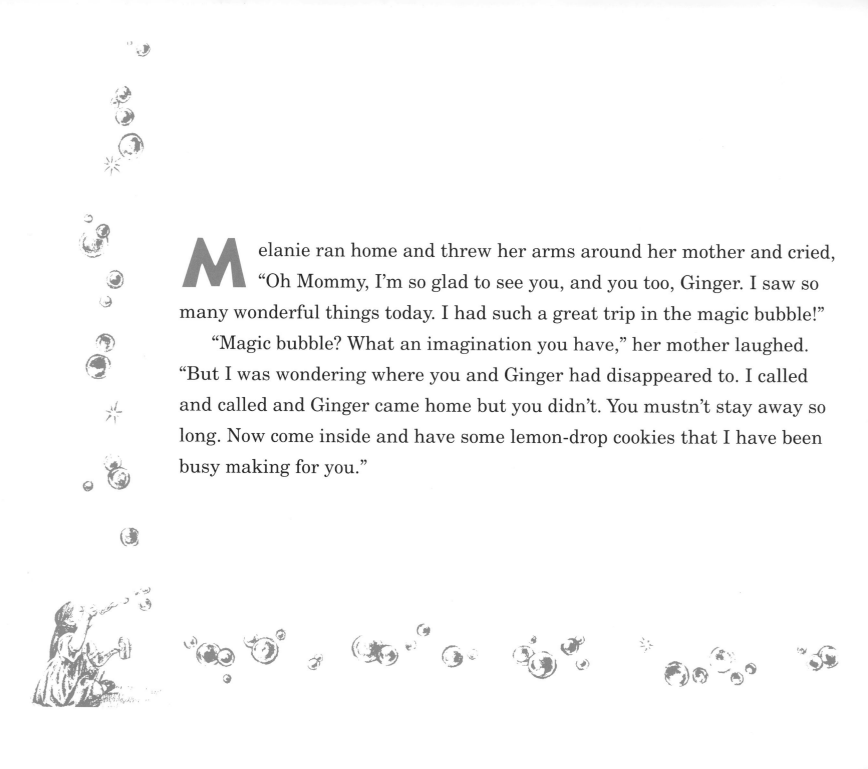

Melanie ran home and threw her arms around her mother and cried, "Oh Mommy, I'm so glad to see you, and you too, Ginger. I saw so many wonderful things today. I had such a great trip in the magic bubble!"

"Magic bubble? What an imagination you have," her mother laughed. "But I was wondering where you and Ginger had disappeared to. I called and called and Ginger came home but you didn't. You mustn't stay away so long. Now come inside and have some lemon-drop cookies that I have been busy making for you."

Ever after, Melanie spent a lot of time looking at things, reading books, and learning about the world around her. She was curious about everything, and nothing was ever quite the same after that magical day. And sometimes, if she felt just a little bit mumfy, she and Ginger would sit on the grass and look up into the sky and watch the clouds. And yes, sometimes, if she looked ever so carefully, she was sure she caught a glimpse of Mrs. Huggins smiling down at her.

6496 Youngs Road, Winlaw, B.C., V0G 2J0
and
2758 Charles Street, Vancouver, B.C., V5K 3A7

Published with the assistance of the Canada Council and the British Columbia Cultural Services Branch

Book design by Sandra Robinson
Author photograph by Tom Sutherland
Printed in Canada by Friesen Printers

Canadian Cataloguing in Publication Data
Docksteader, Mary Houghton,
Melanie and the magic bubble

ISBN 0-919591-66-3

I. Title
PS8557.034M4 1993   jC813'.54   C93-091317-5
PZ7.D62Me 1993